Beauty and the Beast

The Tantalising Tales Collection

Lorelei Johnson

A Beauty and the Beast Retelling

Copyright © 2020 Lorelei Johnson

All rights reserved.

The characters and events portrayed in this book are fictitious. Any similarity to real persons, living or dead, is coincidental and not intended by the author.

No part of this book may be reproduced, or stored in a retrieval system, or transmitted in any form or by any means, electronic, mechanical, photocopying, recording, or otherwise, without express written permission of the publisher.

Cover design by: Lorelei Johnson

ISBN: 9798467475806

PROLOGUE

Alaric

Alaric entered the ballroom, the party already in full swing to celebrate his birthday. It had taken a full week for the servants to decorate the room to his mother's vision and it was now packed full of people in their best attire who were probably too drunk to take much notice their surroundings. As he looked around the room, he wasn't sure he knew even half of them. It seemed that his mother had invited all the eligible ladies in the kingdom for the occasion. She wasn't forcing his marriage, she always said she wanted him to marry for love, a thing his father never would have allowed if he was alive. But that didn't mean she wasn't going to try to help the process along wherever she could.

Still, her meddling was relatively harmless, so Alaric didn't mind.

He knew that he would have to marry one day, but like his mother he hoped it would be for love, not duty. Sometimes he imagined what that woman might be like but he'd never been in love before, at least, he didn't think so. Surely it was the sort of feeling one recognised instinctively.

He noticed a woman staring at him across the room. It wasn't that she was the only one doing so, in fact the eyes of just about every woman in the room were fixed on him, but she was different. There was an intensity in her eyes that unnerved him. She was beautiful, he supposed, with her silvery hair intricately woven with jewels, her pale smooth skin, even her figure could not be faulted. She wore the finest dress in the room, rich, expensive fabric that glittered under the lights and other men were eying her lustfully, but there was something about her that made the hair on the back of his neck stand on end.

He tore his eyes away and approached his mother, as he ought to do upon entering the party, glad to have an excuse not to approach the woman. The queen smiled warmly at him and held out her hand to him, as she had done since he was a child. 'Happy birthday, darling.'

'Thank you, mother,' Alaric said, taking her hand. 'You've outdone yourself. How many women can you fit in a single ballroom?'

The queen laughed and waved her hand dismissively. 'I fear that if I left it all to you, you would be single long after I am dead.'

He could feel the strange woman's eyes burning into his back. 'Mother, do you know who that woman is? The one with the silver hair?' he asked, dropping his voice low.

His mother's eyes widened for a moment before she looked back at her son. 'I did not think she would come,' she said, almost to herself. 'Her name is Belladonna. You aren't…' She trailed off as the colour drained from her face, as if she couldn't bear to finish that sentence.

'Aren't what?'

'You aren't thinking of marrying her?' His mother seemed to struggle to get the words out. He'd never known her to be afraid of anyone before and yet she appeared to be afraid of this woman. Had she invited her out of fear? He could think of no other explanation and he couldn't shake that burning question; who was she?

'No,' Alaric said honestly and his mother visibly relaxed. 'She just keeps staring at me, so I was curious.'

Curious was a nice way to put it. She was creeping him out. Women had been brazen with him before, of course they had, he was the prince, but none had ever looked at him like they could devour his soul.

'Stay away from her. She's more dangerous than she seems.' She squeezed his hand tightly before releasing him. It was a sign he should mingle with his guests.

He looked over his shoulder. Belladonna's eyes

were still trained on him and she flashed him a bright and flawless smile. He smiled back awkwardly, out of politeness, before turning away from her again. He wasn't sure how he was going to stay away from her when she seemed so intent on getting his attention, but he certainly did not need to be told twice. He would do everything possible to stay away from Belladonna.

After hours of dancing and drinking, Alaric had almost grown used to the gaze of that strange woman, Belladonna. It was easier to ignore her the longer he kept at it, but he wondered if it was really the best course of action if she was as dangerous as his mother believed. It was strange to think of someone so petite, so delicate as being dangerous, but there was definitely an air of power surrounding her. He supposed she might do something drastic if she felt slighted, although maybe he was thinking too much into it. Dangerous and crazy did not always go hand in hand.

Still, he had no desire to speak with her. Perhaps he was overthinking the whole thing. He hoped she would quickly lose interest and he'd never have to see her again.

People began to file out of the room as the sky began to lighten in the predawn hours. Alaric was glad, it had been a long night and he was ready to get some sleep and finally have a reprieve from Belladonna's staring. But the woman seemed intent to linger. There were only a handful of people left and there she stood, on her own, staring at him with that same intensity in eyes which seemed much too old for her face.

Alaric decided to take his leave instead. He exited the ballroom, breathing a sigh of relief. But his relief was short lived. A small hand slipped into his own and he turned, startled, to find Belladonna staring up at him.

'Pardon me, madam, you seem to have confused me with someone else,' Alaric said awkwardly, trying to retrieve his hand from her clutches.

'I have not, your highness. I have been watching you all night,' she said, a flirtatious lilt to her voice.

'Have you?' he asked. Pretending that he hadn't noticed seemed like the best course of action, even though it would have been impossible not to notice.

'I don't blame you for being oblivious, men often are in situations such as this,' she said, smiling sweetly.

'Situations such as what?'

'Why, love, of course,' she said and giggled, the sound much too sickly sweet for it to feel genuine or good. It sent a shiver up Alaric's spine.

'Love? I'm quite sure we've never met,' Alaric said, a sinking feeling settling in the pit of his stomach.

'How can you be so unfeeling?' she asked, a pout on her lips. 'What about love at first sight?'

'Look, I'm...flattered but I don't believe in love at first sight.'

'Then let's get to know each other, you'll grow to love me, I can feel it.'

'I think you've had too much wine,' Alaric said, trying to disentangle himself from this bizarre woman but her grip was like iron.

'Are you rejecting me, Prince?' She spat the last word like it disgusted her and the air began to change around her, swirling as it had no right to. Behind her sweet façade, something dark and menacing began to show itself.

'What are you doing?' Alaric demanded, snatching his hand away from her, successfully this time, but he couldn't help feeling that was due more to her than his own strength. His blood ran cold at the sight of her now, her hair whipping around her in the strange breeze. A chilling power emanated from her and a crazed look dominated her eyes.

'If you will not love me, then I will ensure no one will ever love you,' she said coldly. 'I curse you to live as the cold-hearted monster you have proven yourself to be.'

'No!' the queen shouted as she ran for her son.

But it was too late.

Alaric cried out in pain as his heart stopped in his chest, the blood flowing through his veins felt like ice, a strange freezing but burning sensation spread through him, the pain was unbearable and he collapsed to his knees.

Belladonna began to laugh as she watched her curse take hold of him. She vanished into thin air, leaving only the echoes of her deranged cackle behind her.

The pain subsided but something burned inside him, a thirst so powerful he gasped against the pain of it searing his throat. He could smell the dampness of the stones, the flowers in the next room, his mother's perfume, the warm blood pumping through the veins of the man approaching him. His words barely registered, a muffled white-noise against the pounding of his heart, the thing he craved gently pumping beneath soft, warm flesh, so close now.

'Stay back!' Alaric managed to shout, his voice broken, husky, almost a growl.

Two guards held the queen back while a third approached Alaric despite his warning. The man leaned down, exposing his neck. The vein was pulsing beneath his skin and before he even knew what he was about to do, Alaric sank his teeth into it, sucking warm blood into his mouth, feeling the relief from the pain as it washed down his throat. When he realised what he was doing, he released the man, his body falling to the floor.

He'd stopped too late. The man was dead.

Alaric looked up at his mother, the horror in her eyes mirroring his own. 'What's happening to me?'

The queen looked at her son with horror and tears began to well in her eyes. She had never looked at him life that before. Oh god, what had he done? What had Belladonna done to him? He didn't know what he was supposed to do but he knew he couldn't stay here, he'd be putting everyone in danger.

The queen squared her shoulders and schooled her expression. 'We can fix this,' she said, 'I need Delphine. Find Delphine!'

'I am here, my queen,' a woman's voice called soothingly. She stepped forward from the shadows dressed in an emerald-green gown. Her chestnut hair dropped gently down her back and there was a warmth in her dark eyes as she took in the scene before her. He could somehow sense the power from her, similar to Belladonna's but the two were as different as day and night.

'Please, Delphine, save my son,' the queen begged.

'I cannot undo the curse of another witch, but I can alter it,' she said. She handed Alaric a dead rosebush planted in an intricate silver pot. His brow furrowed and he looked at her questioningly. 'The woman who can make the roses bloom, only she can lift this curse from you.'

'How can I find her?'

'You cannot,' she smiled sadly. 'Belladonna has done more than curse you to this form. You cannot leave these grounds.'

'Then I will find her for him,' the queen said, squaring her shoulders in determination. 'We'll scour the kingdom until we find her.'

Delphine only shook her head. 'She may not even exist yet. And to protect Alaric, I must wipe him from your memories. No one must ever know he's here. It will be as if he never existed.'

'No! I called you here to help him,' the queen shouted. 'This is not helping him!'

'It's okay, mother. I can't leave this place, and I'm a danger to everyone here. I will be alright,' Alaric said, offering a smile to his mother that he hoped was comforting. 'How will she lift the curse?'

'She must fall in love with you. If she can love you despite your new form, the curse will be broken.'

Hopelessness set in as Delphine's words settled in his mind. His only hope was that a woman would stumble upon him by chance and love him despite his monstrous form. But who could ever love a beast?

CHAPTER 1

Alaric

Alaric stared out into the night, the full moon shining a beautiful silvery light across the still and silent grounds of the castle. Beautiful, cold, and dark, just like he was, an eternal reminder of the monster he had become.

This night marked the hundredth year of his curse. A hundred years of solitude, a hundred years of waiting for a woman to break his curse, but none ever came. Delphine might have thought she was helping but in truth she might have given out the cruellest punishment of all.

All because he didn't love a witch he had never met before.

A movement caught his eye, a human stumbling in the darkness and for a moment his heart leapt to his throat. But it was just a man. The first living soul he'd seen in a century and it was a man, probably stumbling drunk in the night.

He let out a weary sigh.

What was he still doing here? The only person who ever came to this place was Belladonna. She came once a year, maybe it was more often in the beginning, he hardly remembered anymore. Each year she said the same thing. 'If you only agree to be mine, I will lift the curse I placed upon you.'

He knew he would never give in to her but there were other ways to end his curse. The sunlight would easily cure his condition, he wouldn't survive it but it was a way out. And really, what was the point now? Everyone he had ever known was dead, he had no kingdom to rule anymore. He probably wouldn't even recognise the world he stepped into.

And yet he couldn't seem to take that final step.

The man knocked at the door, the rusted old knockers requiring significant effort to move after all those years of being left to the elements. After some minutes, he gave up and pushed the door open instead. 'Hello?' he called out. 'I've lost my way and hoped I might warm myself by the fire for an hour or two.'

The fire in the nearest room spurred to life of its own accord. The man was startled, rightfully so. There were not many enchanted castles in the world, at least, there hadn't been when he was free, and he assumed the same was true even now.

The castle was Delphine's doing. She enchanted it so that it could provide him anything he asked for. Anything except the one thing he truly needed.

The man moved cautiously towards the flames and Alaric let out a sigh. He wasn't keen on the man staying but he supposed he could let him be for an hour, provided he didn't touch anything or stay longer than he should.

The man looked around the room, surprised that no one was there. He sat by the fire, letting it warm his frozen body. He seemed in awe of his surroundings and he had the look of a man concocting a scheme. Did he think the castle was abandoned? He would have the fright of his life if he thought to move in. Alaric would let the man warm himself, but his generosity would go no further. Why should he afford kindness to anyone when he had suffered so at the hands of others?

The man looked around him again before saying, 'Sure would be nice to have something hot to eat.'

The audacity. But as was its function, the castle obeyed and a hot meal appeared next to the man, complete with a glass of beer. Alaric shook his head. Did it need to be quite so good at its job? How was he going to get this wretch out of his castle if the castle was making him feel so comfortable?

Sufficiently warmed and fed, the man finally stood. He stretched his arms wide and took one final look around before heading back out into the night. Alaric watched as he crossed the grounds but he stopped before a rosebush, his mother's rosebush, the one she cherished above all others, the one he had allowed to grow wild and unruly in her absence. She would be appalled if she could see it now.

The man reached out and plucked the last rose in bloom. Alaric's rage blindsided him and before he knew what he was doing, he stood before the man, a snarl on his lips. 'You would steal from me after the generosity I showed you?'

The man fell to the ground in shock, the rose falling from his hand. 'Please, I'm sorry. I didn't think anyone lived here.'

Alaric grabbed the man by his collar, hoisting him up with superhuman strength. The man whimpered, his face turning white with fear, his hands clutching at Alaric's as if he had any hope of freeing himself from the vice-like grip.

'Please, don't kill me,' he begged like a man who was used to begging. He was clearly a scoundrel, and it had been a long time since he'd drunk from the source. Even in the dark of night he could see the vein throbbing in the man's neck, he was so close he could almost taste it. One flick of his finger and he would slice that vein open. The thirst began to burn at his throat.

'Give me one reason I should not,' Alaric growled.

'I-I have a daughter,' the man began. Alaric almost rolled his eyes at the absurdity of the plea, as if that would be enough to save his life. His daughter was probably better off without him. 'If you let me go, you can have her,' the man continued.

Alaric's brow furrowed and he was almost disgusted enough to rip his throat out then and there.

But.

This was the first spark of hope he'd had in a hundred years. It was unlikely the man would keep his word but if she was the one who could free him from his curse, could he risk not taking the chance?

He dropped the man to the ground and he scrambled away. Alaric considered him carefully. He was definitely not an honest man, the only way to ensure he would keep his word would be to scare him so thoroughly that he could do nothing but obey.

'If you are lying to me, I will hunt you down and kill you so slowly that you will beg for death long before I grant it,' he growled, showing his fangs for good measure.

'I'm not lying,' the man said quickly. 'I'm not. I'll bring her to you tomorrow night.'

Alaric nodded. 'Very well. Run, before I change my mind.'

The man scurried away, stumbling several times before disappearing from view. Alaric smiled to himself. The man had no way of knowing that Alaric couldn't leave the castle grounds but it was a chance he had to take.

Tomorrow night, he could be meeting the woman

who could bring an end to all of this. He picked up the rose the man had forgotten in his fear, twirling the flower between his fingers, and he wondered what this woman might be like as he headed back inside the castle. For the first time in a hundred years, he had hope.

CHAPTER 2

Belle

Belle's father was off somewhere again. She didn't bother asking him anymore, chances were he was lying, and if he was telling the truth, she didn't want to know. Ignorance was bliss, as they say, or at least plausible deniability was.

When she was a child he used to tell her he was a merchant, and she supposed he was of sorts. He was a thief and a liar and he was always getting himself into trouble. Always dragging her into it, too. But she had little choice. Her mother had left when she was just a little thing, left her to her fate.

They'd been in town for almost twelve months now, a new record, as far as she could remember. It was a small town, though, and small towns were the most boring. There was nothing to entertain and one had to make their own amusements, which did not always turn out as you planned, as Belle was beginning to learn the hard way.

Bended on one knee, smiling up at her with what passed for a debonaire smile in these parts, Gaston held out a ring which was entirely too big to be anything other than a show of wealth. Well, she wouldn't have expected anything less from him, he was the kind of man who only accepted the best, and the best, to him, was the most beautiful or the most expensive.

Belle tried to smile but it was more like a grimace as her eyes darted around for an out. How had she gotten herself into this mess? It was only supposed to be a bit of fun and now he'd spoiled it all. He was pretty but there wasn't a whole lot going on upstairs.

'Belle, will you marry me?' the words slipped off his tongue full of confidence, as if she could not possibly have any other answer but yes.

The tavern had fallen silent as all the patrons – which was almost everyone in town – looked on with keen interest. Either they were going to have a wedding or they were going to witness a spectacular rejection. Either way, it was going to be entertaining.

For them.

'I…uh,' Belle stammered, unsure how she could let him down gently and also make him understand what she was saying. Who was she kidding? He didn't have enough sense for both. She sighed. 'Gaston, I can't marry you.'

The smile fell from his face and a dumbfounded expression took its place. 'Why? Is it your father? I'm sure he would agree.'

Yes, he probably would, so she was glad he wasn't in town for this particular show. 'I'm not ready to marry anyone.' Not from that village, anyway.

'I can wait.'

God, would this man please just take a hint? She was going to lose her temper and say something she couldn't take back. 'Gaston, please. I won't marry you,' she said sternly and turned on her heels, leaving the tavern as a chorus of laughter erupted behind her. She could just imagine his stupid face, the embarrassment of being laughed at would spark his temper and she wasn't stupid enough to hang around for that. She was going to pay for it later but what else was she supposed to do? At least he would have calmed down somewhat by then, and she took solace in that fact that he was easily distracted, like a raven with shiny objects. It wouldn't be hard to turn his thoughts to other things.

Once she was outside, she almost ran home. She needed to put as much distance between herself and Gaston as was humanly possible. She burst through the door, shutting it firmly behind her and leaning against it with a heavy sigh. She should have known better than to involve herself with a man like Gaston. He was a little stupid – okay, a lot stupid – and incredibly self-absorbed but handsome enough to be a pleasant – and temporary – distraction. Or so she'd thought. How had he gotten it into his thick head that she was in love with him? He certainly wasn't in love with her, though he undoubtedly thought he was. He only wanted her because she was the most beautiful woman in town and he felt that he deserved nothing less.

She needed a bath.

She had moved plenty of times at her father's request, maybe now he would move at hers. Doubtful but worth a try. If he ever came back.

Her father had been gone for three days longer than he should have, and while she would like to think that he had some modicum of fatherly affection in his selfish body, she knew better than to hope for such things. If he didn't return, there was a fifty percent chance he was lying in a ditch somewhere, a victim of his own scheming, and a fifty percent chance that he'd decided to cut his losses and leave her to fend for herself.

Either scenario would likely mean she would have to marry Gaston out of necessity. She shuddered at the thought.

Just as that heinous thought crossed her mind, the door burst open and her father stumbled in, half frozen to death. 'Papa? What in the world?'

He slammed the door shut, his chest heaving with every breath. He was white as a ghost as he strode towards the cupboard, banging and clanging until he found what he was after. His hands shook violently as he poured a glass of whiskey, spilling most of it onto the floor, though he acted as though he hadn't even noticed. He downed the liquid in a single gulp and poured another.

'What happened?' she asked. A bad feeling was beginning to settle in her stomach as she watched his frantic behaviour.

'Get your coat, we need to go.'

Ordinarily, she might have asked questions but she was actually glad to be leaving this time so she grabbed her coat without complaint and followed him into the night.

CHAPTER 3

Belle

The forest was dark and Belle could hear wolves howling somewhere in the distance, the sound sending a shiver up her spine. She wrapped her coat tightly around her as though the lush fabric could protect her from more than the cold.

Her father was acting strange. Well, stranger than usual. Normally, he came home from what he called work and he would give her a gift, a trinket of some sort. It was something that used to delight her as a child but now it felt empty, like a payoff. After that, he would quickly head out to the tavern. Even when he was running from something there was always time for a drink, always time to pack. What on Earth could he have done this time? Who had inspired so much fear in him?

He was muttering to himself as they walked, but

she couldn't make out the words. Maybe he had finally cracked, maybe she should have asked more questions at home and called the asylum.

'What's going on, papa?' Belle asked, unable to keep quiet any longer.

'I'll explain later. Come on, we don't have much time,' he said quickly. He looked around then picked up his pace, forcing her to scramble to keep up with him. Was he running from danger or from her questions? Either was entirely possible.

'Much time for what?' she persisted.

He began muttering to himself again. Every now and then he would stop and look around him as if he wasn't sure where he was going, before finally setting off again with renewed purpose.

'Papa, please, where are we going?' Belle asked, frustration strangling her words. Her feet ached against the bitter cold of melted snow that soaked through her shoes. She had wanted to get away from Gaston but she wasn't sure this was worth it. It felt like she had jumped out of the frying pan and into the fire.

'Not far now, Belle, not far. We're going to be all right, everything is going to be alright,' her father answered, but she couldn't help feeling that his words were meant to comfort himself, not her. His selfishness never ceased to amaze, although she had thought it would hurt less by now.

Finally, the trees began to recede and in the distance she could see an austere castle, its turrets and towers ghostly and strange in the pale moonlight. She found herself looking around, searching for some other reason they might be headed in this direction. Surely this creepy place was not her father's intended destination? But as they got closer and closer to the structure, there was little room left for doubt.

'Papa?' she asked. Her voice sounded small to her own ears and suddenly she felt like a child again.

Her father didn't answer. As they drew closer, Belle began to make out an ornate stone doorway gaping like a great mouth. In the centre of that doorway, a man stood with folded arms, watching their approach. She couldn't make out his features fully in the darkness, but he was tall and lean, and unnaturally still. Her father stiffened at the sight of him; he was clearly a formidable man to strike fear so decidedly into her father, who prided himself on being able to get out of any situation.

'My lord, I've done as I promised,' her father said. 'I've brought my daughter.'

'You what? Papa, what have you done?' she demanded, all fear dissipating as fury took over. For all her father's schemes and underhanded dealings, Belle had never once thought that she would be just another tool for him to exploit. Not like this.

'Belle, don't look at your papa like that,' he father pleaded. He moved to stroke her hair the way he used to do when she was a child, but she smacked his hand away.

The lord, who had been watching the scene with a look of disinterest, turned his to her, his eyes briefly raking over her body before coming to settle on her face. He held her gaze for a moment that felt like an eternity and her breath hitched in her throat. It wasn't fear she felt as she stared into those dark eyes but something else, something more, something she shouldn't be feeling at a time like this.

Now that she was closer, she could see pale skin that looked almost ghostly in the moonlight, prominent cheekbones and a strong jawline without a hint of stubble. There was something about him that drew her in, that stirred a curiosity in her. Who was this man?

Finally, he looked away and the spell was broken.

'Is somebody going to tell me what the hell is going on?' Belle demanded as she focused once again on her anger, attempting to ignore the strange feelings this man had awakened in her with a single look. 'Who the hell are you?'

The lord raised an eyebrow at her in that way men often did around women they thought were being hysterical. 'Your father tried to steal something from me,' he said. 'He offered a boon in exchange for his life.'

Belle didn't know who she was more shocked at, her father or this lord. 'What kind of man asks for a woman he doesn't even know as compensation?' she asked. It was the least painful of the two questions burning in her mind.

'I did not ask for you,' the lord said dismissively, which stung strangely like rejection in her chest. Her father dropped his eyes to his feet. 'He offered you of his own volition.'

'Papa?' Belle asked, turning her fury once again on her father.

'B-Belle, you have to understand…' but he didn't continue; he clearly didn't know how to justify his actions this time, which suited her just fine. She was in no mood to hear his excuses.

'You offered up your daughter to a man who was going to kill you, to save yourself. Just what is it you think he's going to do with me?' Belle asked, balling her hands into fists. Her father would not look at her. He had no words for the daughter he had just sacrificed. 'You are a despicable excuse for a man, Maurice,' she said, choosing the words she knew would hurt him the most, the same words her mother had used before she left them. But nothing could compare to the hurt he had inflicted on her.

Belle squared her shoulders and marched toward the lord, her head held high. She did not turn back to see her father. As far as she was concerned, she no longer had a father. He led her inside and Belle made sure her mask was firmly in place, as if she was playing a game of poker. She would not let this man see her weakness.

The castle was dark, only a few candles dimly

lighting the huge dwelling. He picked up a lantern. 'Follow me,' he said, leaving her no time to take in her surroundings.

He led her down a long hallway, the candlelight dancing with the shadows. Belle swallowed hard, tightening her arms around herself once more. She felt like she had wandered into a nightmare that she could wake from at any moment if only she could open her eyes. Unshed tears pricked at her eyes as she wondered what was going to happen to her, but she quickly shook her head to get rid of them. She could cry when she was alone.

Never let them see you cry. It was one of the few lessons her mother had taught her before she left.

'Are you going to keep me in the dungeon?' she asked, breaking the silence.

'Would you like to be kept in the dungeon?' he asked, amusement dancing in his voice.

'Not especially,' Belle mumbled irritably.

They stopped in front of a huge door that was on the extravagant side of decency. At least it didn't look like the door to a dungeon. He opened it and held the lantern out to her. She hesitated for a moment before she took it from him and stepped into the room. She looked around but could see very little in the dim light. She could just make out the looming silhouette of a fourposter bed and a few other furnishings. The kind of things you might expect to find in a guest bedroom.

'Who are you?' she asked, turning back to him. She

searched his face as though she might find the answers there if she looked hard enough. She hadn't even known there was a castle so close to town, let alone that it might be occupied. How had he concealed himself to thoroughly from the world?

'My name is Alaric,' he said. That seemed to be the end of his pleasantries and Belle wondered how long it had been since he had been around people. She knew beggars with better manners. 'You are free to roam the castle and the grounds as you like, I don't really care what you do while you are here. But you will remain on the grounds and you are not to enter the west wing. Unless you wish to move to the dungeons,' he continued, his voice showing no hint of emotion.

How many times he had given this speech? How many girls had been in her place before? What fate had her father thrown her into?

She forced herself to calm down. Panicking would get her nowhere now. She needed to stay focused. 'Why can't I go in the west wing?

But he simply looked at her coldly and slammed the door shut, leaving her alone in this strange place. She didn't hear the click of a lock, so she assumed it was open, but where would she go if she left? It would be suicide to try and escape now.

She put the lantern on the bedside table and crawled into the enormous bed. It smelled old and musty and she let her tears fall freely until sleep finally claimed her.

CHAPTER 4

Alaric

The woman, Belle her father called her, was beautiful, more beautiful than he had ever imagined. Her golden hair cascaded down her long, slender neck, her smooth porcelain skin almost glowed in the moonlight, her lips were plump and red, her eyes sparkled with a fierceness that lay beneath that perfect surface. If any woman was like the ocean, she must be it.

He wasn't sure if Belle was her real name or a nickname she'd been given after her beauty. Either could be entirely possible. He should have asked her, he should have said something, anything. He had never beheld such a beautiful creature in his life, not even before the curse, and that quashed the hope that had dared to flicker to life in his heart. How could a woman like her ever come to love a monster?

Especially when that monster hadn't even bothered to ask her name.

He sighed.

It had been a century since he'd been around a woman. He didn't know what he'd been expecting, exactly. Someone dainty and good, someone with less beauty, with less fire, someone easier for him to be around. He had no idea how to be around Belle. She filled him with a desire like he had never known and yet he could not touch her, he could barely speak to her. He'd shown her to her room and runaway like a coward.

A woman like that would not appreciate being caged and there he stood as her jailer. He needed a way to get her to look past that, somehow.

What did women like? Jewellery? He only had to wish it and it would appear but while the gesture might be well-meaning, she could take insult to it. Dancing? It wasn't as if he could host a ball for her, no one even knew he existed. Flowers? He could summon a bouquet but the flowers in the garden had all died for the winter.

Damn it. Why didn't he know what to do? His salvation was at hand and he had no idea how to grab it.

He could hear her sobbing quietly into her pillow from her room and a twinge of guilt flicked him. He definitely could have been more…comforting. Her father had just betrayed her and now she was locked in a strange place with a man she didn't know. She had handled it so well, she looked so strong, he hadn't even suspected that it might all be a façade. What kind of life must she have had with a father like that?

He let out a frustrated sigh and moved towards the window where the dead rosebush sat in its glittering silver pot. He scanned every gnarled, thorny branch but it was as dead as it ever was. When would he know if she was the one? How long would this thing take to bloom? He should have asked more questions about that, too. Was it supposed to bloom as soon as she entered the castle? Did she need to come into contact with it? Or would it only bloom after she had fallen in love with him?

The rosebush offered no answers and the pot glittered happily in the moonlight as if it were mocking him.

The sobbing finally stopped, Belle had obviously cried herself to sleep. Maybe he could find a way to make it up to her tomorrow. He would need to think of some way to show her it wasn't all bad in this place, even though he had long ago forgotten the pleasures that could be had there. How was one supposed to make their prison look appealing enough for another person to move in?

The sun began to peak over the horizon. Even after a hundred years, he still dreaded the sunrise. It was yet another reminder of what he was; a fucking monster. He pulled the curtains closed and walked to the bookcase, pulling a single book down with a mechanical click. It had seemed pointless, in the beginning, hiding away in the daylight hours when no one even knew he existed. It didn't seem likely anyone was going to come to murder him, and he had thought once or twice that such a reprieve wouldn't be entirely unwelcome. Now it had become habit.

The bookcase swung open to reveal a hidden room; it was small with just enough space for a bed. He pulled the concealed door shut behind him and prepared to sleep out the day. He hoped that Belle wouldn't get into too much trouble while he slept. He wondered if she would even be there when he woke.

CHAPTER 5

Belle

When Belle woke, the sun was already low in the sky, painting the world in hues of orange and yellow. She rubbed her bleary eyes. Had she really slept the entire day? She pulled herself out of the musty bed and opened the closet. Inside, she flipped through a dozen dresses, all of them beautiful and of the best quality, all of them in her size. Lord Alaric had clearly prepared for her arrival, just how much had her father told him about her? He had a room for her, and clothes, did Alaric really intend to keep her prisoner for the rest of her life?

It didn't really feel like she was a prisoner, more like a guest to a grumpy host. A guest who couldn't leave, but that wasn't too different to being a lady in most situations. Men dictated what women could and couldn't do every day.

For now, she supposed she would explore the mysterious castle no one seemed to know about. If she was going to escape one day, it would be better to know the lay of the land, as it were.

She pulled one of the gowns on. It was a little more modest than she would have chosen for herself, but her choices were limited. She slipped on some shoes and decided to start her exploration with the kitchens.

She wandered the halls for forty minutes, entering room after room of the enormous castle, only to find it completely empty. She hadn't come across a single person, not even Lord Alaric. He couldn't live in this place alone, could he? It was the sort of place that couldn't run without an army of people taking care of it, and yet, despite the layer of dust that seemed to coat almost everything, it was perfectly orderly and clean.

Her stomach rumbled loudly. She was starving but she had yet to find the kitchen. 'What does a girl have to do to get some food around here?' she grumbled under her breath.

She caught a delectable scent wafting through the air, which had definitely not been there before and followed it as her stomach rumbled again. It led her to a ridiculous sized double door and she pushed one open, grunting under the weight of it. Her eyes lit up at the sight of the enormous varnished table set for one with an array of intricate dishes on display; far too much food for one person to consume. The spread must have taken the kitchen staff hours to prepare and yet, the castle had been completely silent. Where were the cooks, the servers, anyone? She was certain that Lord Alaric hadn't prepared the food, and she definitely couldn't picture him cleaning hallways and scrubbing floors. Someone else had to be there. Why were they hiding? Was Alaric that terrifying?

'Hello?' she called out into the empty space as she looked around her, but there was no answer. Had the food been set out for her or the master of the castle? It would be incredibly rude of him not to feed her and, as there was far too much food for one person, she doubted it would matter if she had a little bite to eat.

Taking one last look around, Belle sat at the table and filled her plate. She hadn't realised how hungry she was until she took that first bite, and she ate her fill rather too quickly to be considered ladylike. She was grateful that she was alone, although there was something unsettling about being so alone in such a large place.

'Well, now what am I going to do?' she asked the empty room and sighed.

I don't really care what you do while you are here. But you will remain on the grounds and you are not to enter the west wing.

She drummed her fingers on the table, the sound echoing loudly in the silent room. Why bother keeping her here if he didn't care what she did? And why was the west wing the only place that was off limits? What was he hiding up there?

She stood up and headed out into the hallway once more. She looked left, then right and realised that she couldn't remember which way she'd come in. Well, it wasn't like she was running out of time to find her way. She might actually die of boredom before anything else.

Of course, the best way to stave off that boredom might just be to find out what was in a forbidden wing in a creepy old castle nobody knew about. It might come with death by a terrifying loner lord but it wouldn't be boring.

Yeah, okay, it was a stupid idea.

There had to be something to do in this place.

She stopped suddenly, finding herself at the foot of an enormous, curved staircase, lined with ornate bannisters carved with twirling vines. The stair runner was a lush red fringed with woven white blooms, a stark contrast to the dark mahogany beath it. Beyond the stairs, everything was shrouded in a thick darkness, as if someone had taken great pains to keep every spec of light away from this place.

Could this be the forbidden west wing? She'd never been very good with directions, she could simply tell Alaric that she got lost, that she didn't know. It wasn't like he'd handed her a map or hung a 'do not enter' sign. Besides, what more could he do to her?

Well, he could throw her in the dungeon, she supposed. That would be less appealing than her current situation. But he would have to forgive her eventually, and if she'd learnt anything from her father, it was that it was better to ask for forgiveness than permission.

She placed her hand on the railing, a giddy excitement stirring within her, the kind that only comes from doing something you're not supposed to. Of course, the surest way to get Belle to do anything was to tell her she couldn't – a trait she was well aware of.

She took one step onto the staircase when a voice stopped her in her tracks. 'Didn't I tell you not to enter the west wing?'

She swallowed hard and looked up to see Lord Alaric stepping out of the shadows. There was a warning in his eyes. She hadn't thought she'd be caught so quickly. How long had he been watching her?

'Oh, so this is the west wing. I had no idea,' she said, doing her best to sound apologetic.

He arched an unamused eyebrow at her. 'You know, somehow I thought you'd be a better liar.'

'That's rude,' she said, crossing her arms over her chest and jutting out her hip.

'Am I wrong?'

'Maybe I was lonely in this big, empty castle all by myself,' Bell said innocently. How many times had she played dumb to get what she wanted? Men were so easily led, losing all their senses in a pretty face.

'If you wanted to see me,' he said, his voice a low rumble. Suddenly, he was just inches from her and she gasped. He placed a finger under her chin, tilting her head up. 'All you had to do was ask.'

How had he moved so quickly? He was...it wasn't possible. She raised her head, determined to show him that she didn't scare so easily, even as her mind was screaming for her to run. 'Ask who? There's no one around to ask.'

He smiled to himself. 'You haven't figured it out yet?'

Her brow furrowed. 'Figured what out?'

'The castle is enchanted.'

'So you're, what, a wizard or something?'

Alaric laughed then, the sound echoing through the hall. 'No, I'm not.' He took her hand, and she flinched at the icy touch of his skin. 'Cold hands, sorry,' he said, snatching his hand back. Something dark crossed his eyes and he was back to the stiff lord he'd first presented to her, as if he'd remembered himself and put his mask back into place.

But she wanted to see the man he hid behind that mask. A strange mixture of fear and curiosity swirled inside her and she wasn't sure if she should run from him or stand next to him. What she wanted wasn't always what was good for her.

Alaric continued down the stairs and stood in front of a little table, then beckoned her to follow. Belle did as she was told, her curiosity dancing excitedly in her chest. 'Ask for something.'

'Like what?' she asked, suddenly unsure what she should ask for.

'Anything.'

Alaric watched her with great interest as she considered what to ask for. 'I'd like a rose, please,' she said, her cheeks colouring as embarrassment set in. It felt strange to be requesting something from an enchanted castle and yet Alaric seemed perfectly serious.

She looked up at Alaric questioningly and he nodded towards the little table. Sitting on top of it was a beautiful red rose, the colour more vibrant than she had ever seen before. She gasped in surprise and picked it up, twirling it in her fingers as she examined it. She brought it to her nose and the scent was more beautiful than any rose she had ever smelled before.

'Amazing,' she breathed, still staring at the little flower the castle had given her. 'So there really aren't any servants here?'

'No, the castle does whatever is required.' There was something lonely in his tone that made her heart ache.

'Why do you live here alone?' she asked, suddenly looking up at him.

'That's a complicated question for another time,' he answered wearily. 'Is Belle your real name or a nickname?'

'That's not fair, you won't answer my questions but

I'm supposed to answer yours?' she complained. Alaric simply looked at her, waiting as if he had all the time in the world. She finally sighed. 'Real. I know, it's stupid.'

'I think it's beautiful.'

'Ha ha,' Belle said flatly. Like she'd never heard that one before.

'I'm serious.'

She looked at him closely then, as if she could see past that mask if only she got a little closer. She'd never met anyone like him before. She was aware that she was much too close now but there was something about him that drew her in, something that filled her with a need to know more.

'Ouch,' Belle said as a pain shot through her finger. She clicked her tongue in annoyance, putting the wound to her lips. She'd been so distracted by him that she'd pricked her finger on a thorn.

She looked up to laugh it off, but Alaric was gone. It was as if he had never been there at all.

CHAPTER 6

Alaric

Alaric's chest heaved with every breath as he tried to calm the raging thirst clawing at his throat. He had never had to fight his instincts so hard before. Belle had pricked her finger on that damn rose she's asked for. The scent had been intoxicating, better than anything he'd smelled in a hundred years, and that sickened him. He'd wanted to take her finger and slide it into his mouth, to run his tongue along the wound. He'd imagined what it might taste like as the blood coated his tongue, as it slid down his throat.

If he had done that, she would have thought he was sick, mentally ill maybe. If he had done that, he wasn't sure he would be able to stop. Then she would really know what kind of monster he was. So he'd fled. What else could he do? He would have to apologise later, make some excuse that would be more forgivable, though no matter what he said, he would be lesser in her eyes.

How was he supposed to make her fall in love with him if he couldn't even be around her?

He took a glass of blood off the side table, hoping that it might take the edge off. He should have done it before going to her but he'd been impatient and she'd been so close, it was impossible to resist.

He looked over at the rosebush in its silver pot. Still dead. Maybe she wasn't the one after all. But he wasn't ready to give up yet. If he had to spend another hundred years alone in this castle, he'd rather meet the sun.

'Is he a ghost?' he heard Belle ask herself. She snorted an unladylike sound that made him smile. 'Come on, ghosts now?'

He listened to her footsteps as she walked away. He hadn't expected her to draw him in, but he did like being near her. Maybe it was only because he hadn't been near anyone in such a long time, maybe it was only because she could be the key to his salvation. He really had no way of knowing.

He finished his glass of blood and removed any evidence it may have left on him before he decided to find her again. Her wound would be healed and perhaps now that he was fed, any repeat incidents would not cause such a severe reaction in him. He let out a long breath as he mustered the courage to face her, then headed back down the stairs.

It was easy enough to locate her, funny how any tiny sound was somehow louder in the silence of the empty castle. She was in the library, which he had admittedly not been inside in years. He'd read every book ten times over and given up. He could ask the castle for more books but what would he ask for? He didn't know what was happening in the world while he was trapped inside his time capsule, and the more he read about it, the more resentful he grew of his confinement.

'I see you've discovered the library.'

Belle started and spun around, placing her hand on her racing heart. 'You scared me half to death!'

He shrugged guiltily as he tried not to smile. It wasn't the reaction he'd expected, which he was glad for. 'Sorry.'

'Where did you disappear to before?' she asked, titling her head at him as if he were a curiosity.

'I ah…' he stammered. Shit. He really should have figured out his excuse before he'd come down.

'You don't like blood,' she finished, having apparently come to her own conclusion. She gave a little shrug. 'It's not as uncommon as you might think. But look.' She held up her injured finger for him to see. 'All better.'

'Is this your way of asking me to keep you company?'

A conflicted look settled on her face for a moment

and he desperately wanted to know what she was thinking, and yet he also didn't want to know, afraid of what those thoughts might be. 'Being around you is confusing,' she finally said.

'How?'

'You're keeping me here as a prisoner, although as far as prisons go it is fairly nice. But you're…not the monster I expected you to be.'

Oh, but he was.

'Why did you want me here? And don't tell me it's a complicated question for another time.'

Alaric let out a heavy sigh. He supposed he would have to answer some of her questions if he had any hope of keeping her without physically locking her up. Right now, she didn't know he couldn't go after her if she ran – well, if she ran fast enough. If he told her, would she stay or would she flee as soon as the sun rose?

'I can't leave this place,' he finally admitted. 'The castle was enchanted by a witch and I was trapped here.' Half-truths were better than nothing and he wasn't ready to admit to her what he really was, because then she really would run as soon as the sun rose.

Belle's brow furrowed again. 'So, when my father offered me in his place?'

'I thought it might be nice to have a companion, for a little while, at least,' he said and shrugged awkwardly. Another half-truth. A companion might be nice but it was far from the real reason behind his actions.

'Would you really have killed him?'

He shrugged, a playful smile on his lips. 'Who knows?'

In truth, he probably wouldn't have. He'd killed one man in his life and that was enough for him. He had lost his temper but he likely would have sent him scurrying away, too afraid to ever come back.

She smiled softly at him then, a beautiful sight that caused his heart to squeeze with guilt. 'I don't think you're as bad as you pretend to be.'

If she knew the truth, would she think differently? Would she realise that he was, in fact, worse than she had ever imagined?

'How long have you been here?' she asked.

'It's hard to say, I've lost count,' Alaric said smoothly. Blatant lie. He had counted every single day but if he told her that, then she would ask how he was alive and he didn't want to go there. 'I won't keep you here forever, unless you want to stay.' That was true. He would keep her for just a little while and if the rosebush didn't bloom, he would let her go back to her life. But part of him hoped that she might stay, whether it bloomed or not. He did like having her there.

Her smiled brightened then and she held out a book to him. 'Come and read to me,' she said.

It was a strange request, no one had ever asked him

to read to them…well, not since he was a child taking lessons. He took the book from her and she summoned a fire, clearly still delighting in her new discovery of the castles enchantment. She sat on the rug in front of the flames and Alaric decided to join her, leaning his back against the lounge rather than sitting in it. He opened the book and began to read.

The clock ticked lazily on the mantle, the fire crackled contentedly, and Belle listened for hours. He expected her to tell him to stop but she seemed perfectly happy with the activity. The clock chimed at midnight and he ignored it, as he usually did. Midnight meant nothing to him anymore.

Belle suddenly shifted, moving herself between his legs and resting against his chest. He stiffened, unsure of what he was supposed to do, unsure of what she was doing. 'I won't keep you warm,' he said, and for the first time in a long time that made him sad.

She sighed sleepily, her eyelids already closed. 'The fire will keep me warm. Keep reading, I like the sound of your voice,' she said.

He wasn't sure what he had done to earn this reaction, but whatever it was seemed to be working. At least she wasn't running from him or resenting him for her own imprisonment. Although she probably should be.

'You're not reading,' she mumbled.

He began to read again and he looked down to see a smile on her lips, small and gentle. He doubted he would ever understand her but he wanted to protect her, to keep her. He wasn't even sure it mattered if the rose bloomed anymore.

As he read, her breathing became deeper and her heart slowed to a steady pace. She had fallen asleep. He put aside the book and lifted her into his arms. He never imagined he would be putting her to bed but here he was. How could she be so completely unafraid of him? He tucked her into her bed and watched her sleep for a moment as he remembered the feel of her in his arms.

'You are supposed to fall for me, not the other way around,' he mused. He brushed a lock of hair from her face before forcing himself to leave the room. He could have stayed and watched her all night, but he'd made good progress with her tonight and he didn't want to ruin it.

'Goodnight,' he whispered from the doorway before closing the door softly behind him. How was he supposed to wait until tomorrow night to see her again?

CHAPTER 7

Belle

Belle woke feeling a little more refreshed than she had the day before. She didn't remember going to be last night. The last thing she remembered was Alaric reading to her by the fireplace. A soft smile touched her lips at the memory. He was nothing like she'd though he would be. He was kind, gentle, even. A little awkward at times, sure, but then, he had been alone for who knew how long. It was endearing, really.

She wanted to see him again.

She bathed and changed her clothes as an excitement she hadn't felt in a long time buzzed in her stomach. She raced out the door but only made it only a few steps before she realised that she had no idea where to start looking. Well, that wasn't exactly true. If she was to guess where he would be, there was one place that came to mind, a place that was off limits. She toyed with the idea for a few moments before deciding to explore the rest of the castle first. If she didn't find him, then she would go to the forbidden wing and she would be justified in doing so.

If you wanted to see me, all you had to do was ask.

That wouldn't really work, would it? If she asked the castle would it present him to her? She wasn't willing to try, it seemed ridiculous. If it didn't work, she would feel stupid for trying and if it did she would be embarrassed for another reason entirely.

She would do it the old-fashioned way.

After hours of looking, she had come up empty, as she had expected. She hated the whole process. It was ridiculous to be trapsing around the castle when she knew she wouldn't find him. When had she every played coy for a man?

She took a deep breath, squared her shoulders, and headed for the west wing.

The stairs were the same as before, though somehow they felt more foreboding now. Before she was simply breaking the rules some man had laid down, but this felt more like a betrayal. She chewed her lips as she stared up at the darkness.

'I'd like to see Alaric,' she said softly, embarrassment curling through her. 'Please.'

A lantern at the top of the stairs lit up but nothing else happened. Did that mean she was supposed to go up there? Or was that only her subconscious trying to justify her actions?

She took a deep breath and placed a hand on the railing, her heart racing in nervous anticipation. Slowly she began to climb the stairs, expecting that, as before, Alaric would appear and raise that eyebrow at her.

But he did not.

She reached the top of the stairs and looked around her cautiously before pressing on. The west wing was darker than the rest of the castle, there were no lanterns lit, no candles that she could see, no sunlight peeking through any window. A sense of dread began to creep into her heart and her steps faltered. Maybe she should turn back. It wasn't the most foolish thing she had ever done in her life but she suspected that it was fairly high on that list.

But that burning curiosity would not rest. She wanted to know why Alaric had so specifically forbidden her entering this part of the castle. What was he hiding up here that he didn't want her to find?

She took a deep breath and forced her feet to move again, running her hand along the wall to help her find her way in the darkness. Finally, she could see the soft moonlight up ahead through a door that was slightly ajar. Was Alaric in there after all? She wondered for a moment what he would do if he found her there. Would he really send her to the dungeons or would he do something worse? She could still turn back, call to him from the stairs and pretend that she had never set foot in this place. But she couldn't see him doing any of those things to her. The man she had come to know under that severe exterior was not as he appeared at all.

Better to ask forgiveness than permission, a voice in the back of her head reminded her as curiosity gnawed at her relentlessly. She couldn't turn back now, she had to know. She pushed the door gently, peaking through to make sure the room was empty before stepping inside.

The room was immaculate and sparsely furnished. Old paintings hung on the wall in intricate gold frames, the kind you would expect from an old castle. One was of a couple in wedding attire, royalty, judging from the crowns and the thrones. One was of a family; father, mother, and a boy who was maybe twelve. The boy showed no emotion on his face, and it made him seem older than he was, but there was a hint of sadness in his eyes. The final portrait was of Lord Alaric. He looked the same as he did now, only there was more colour in his complexion and a genuine smile, which she had seen so rarely from the man himself. The painting seemed very old, in an antique frame covered in dust. No. That couldn't be right. Maybe it wasn't Alaric at all, but some relative?

As she moved towards the window, she noticed a dead rosebush. It was planted in an elegant silver pot that sparkled in the moonlight. Why would he keep such a dead thing in something so expensive? As she moved towards the rosebush, a bud began to grow before her eyes. She blinked in surprise but it was still there, a deep crimson red. She was mesmerised as she watched it grew bigger and bigger, then it began to bloom, each petal seeming more vibrant than the last as they unfurled against the moonlight. She reached for it without thinking, filled with a desire to touch the velvet petals when the door suddenly slammed open.

Belle jumped, pulling her hand back as she spun around to see Alaric in the doorway, pure rage set on his face. For the first time since she'd arrived, Belle was truly scared of him. 'What are you doing here?' he snarled.

'I –' Belle started but she could not get the words to leave her throat. The man before her was not at all like the one she knew. There was an anger in him that she had never suspected was lying beneath the goodness she had seen.

'I told you this wing is forbidden!' He moved towards her with an inhuman speed, stopping only inches from her. The movement that had awed her only yesterday now made her heart race for an entirely different reason.

'I know, but I –' she said as she shrank away from him, trying desperately to find the words that would get her out of this. It seemed that in this instance asking permission would have been the better option.

'Get out!' he roared. His eyes were darker than she'd ever seen them and from his lips, she could see fangs protruding. He truly looked like something from a nightmare.

Belle didn't waste a second. She fled from the room, from him. She raced down the stairs, almost tripping over her hems in her haste. She lifted her skirts and raced through the castle to the entrance hall. She pulled open the door and ran into the night. As the cold swirled around her, biting into her skin, she wished she'd grabbed her coat, but there hadn't been time. She only knew that she needed to get out of that place and her feet carried her as fast as they could.

You will remain on the grounds. Unless you wish to move to the dungeons.

Belle stopped suddenly, her feet planted in the snow that had dusted the ground. She wrapped her arms around herself, the cold finally registering through her fear. She looked around her but the forest gave her no sense of where she was or which way she should go.

'You've really done it this time,' she said, chastising herself for her idiocy. She only needed to get off the grounds, then he couldn't follow her. But how far was that? How far had she already come?

The sound of wolves filled the air and her heart began to race. She couldn't tell which direction it was coming from until the wolves finally appeared through the trees in front of her, snarling with vicious teeth.

'Shit,' Belle said as she turned around and broke into a run again, knowing full well there was no way she could outrun the pack but desperately hoping for a miracle, maybe she could get back to the castle or...hell, maybe she was running towards her death and away from it at the same time.

She looked behind her to see the wolves were gaining. She was never going to make it back to the castle. Her foot caught in a root, sending her tumbling down the hill. She landed heavily and the breath rushed out of her lungs. Is this how she was going to die, cold and alone in the snow, torn apart by wolves?

The snarling grew closer and she braced herself for the end. A sickening thud and the snapping of bones sent a shudder through her body and she looked up to see one of the wolves was lying motionless on the ground. The others had their attention focused on a new target.

Alaric.

CHAPTER 8

Alaric

'Fuck!' Alaric growled, sending the contents of the desk crashing to the floor. His hands gripped the table so hard he could hear the wood splintering beneath his fingers. What was she doing in here? He should have known, he should have locked the door to ensure she didn't get this far. How could he be so stupid?

A burst of colour caught his eye and he looked over at the once dead rosebush to see it blooming flowers and growing leaves. He stared at it, frozen in shock. How many times had he stared at that gnarled dead plant? How many times had he cursed Delphine for it? And now it was coming alive because of Belle. She really was his salvation. And he he'd lost his temper and now she was…

Fuck. That wasn't her door closing, it was the front

door. Shit, shit, shit!

Alaric raced through the castle, following her into the snow. Her footprints were easy enough to follow but he heard the distinct howling of wolves. Of all nights, why did they have to be out this one?

He heard Belle scream and pushed himself faster. The pack of wolves were slowly closing in on her as she lay at the bottom of the slope. He could hear her struggling to get her breath back. He grabbed one of the wolves by the tail and threw it with all his strength into a tree. The thing wouldn't die so easily but it would be out for a few hours, at least.

By some miracle, Belle was on the castle grounds, just. He could still reach her, but first he had to deal with the wolves. The pack attacked, fangs and claws, gnashing and slashing. Alaric fought them off easily, it wasn't the first time he'd fought Belladonna's guard dogs and it probably wouldn't be the last. Unless he got bitten.

Claws sliced through his arm and he howled in pain before sending another wolf flying. The wolves surrounded him, growling but not moving. Blood dripped down his arm as he waited for the alpha to present himself, as he surely would.

One of the wolves crouched back on his haunches and leapt, as though he were about the lunge at Alaric, but by the time his paws hit the ground they were no longer paws. His body shifted and twisted as he flew through the air, changing colour and shape, legs lengthening and straightening, until there was not a wolf but a man crouched in the snow. He stood, revealing that he was completely naked. Belle gasped in shock and Alaric glanced at her, even as he knew he shouldn't take his eyes off the wolves, he needed to make sure she was safe. She stared, transfixed at the man's tightly muscled form, his chest covered in coarse dark hair. Alaric would have preferred her to look away. He didn't like her eyes lingering on another man.

Was that jealousy?

'Going somewhere, bloodsucker?' the man spat, his expression fierce as he glared at Alaric.

Alaric raised an eyebrow. 'I am still on my lands, Clayton. And so is the girl.'

Clayton strode forward until there was barely an inch between them. 'Cutting it close, don't you think? Tell me, do you think she is the one, even after all she's seen tonight?'

'It's not really your concern, is it?'

Clayton glanced over at Belle and she met his yellow eyes boldly. Alaric felt a strange sense of pride at her bravery. 'Maybe we'll keep your charge for ourselves,' Clayton leered.

'Try it, if you think you can,' Alaric replied, his voice low and sharp with menace. A thick silence hung heavily in the air as the two men stared each other down, before Clayton finally broke eye contact.

'If I find you on the boarder again, I'll rip out your

throat, leech,' he growled, before turning away. Within a few strides, he was once again on all fours, his grey hair sleek in the moonlight. He led the way into the night, and one by one the other wolves backed away and turned to follow him, disappearing into the dark.

Alaric let out a sigh of relief before looking over at Belle. He could feel his strength fading fast, the slash from Clayton's claws stung viciously. He would live, but he would need time to recover. He needed to get back to the castle to feed. He took a step towards Belle and his legs buckled beneath him.

'Alaric!' Belle shouted and raced to his side. The wound on his arm was bleeding badly, turning the fabric of his shirt a deep red that spread by the second.

'You are more trouble than you look,' he said irritably. But not more trouble than she was worth. He was relieved to find her unharmed, relieved he'd found her in time.

'We have to get you to a doctor,' she said, ignoring his jab. There was genuine concern in her eyes and it eased the anxiety that had been squeezing his heart. Was she not afraid of him anymore? If he was so lucky, he vowed never to lose his temper with her again.

'No,' Alaric said hoarsely. 'Take me back to the castle.'

Belle pulled his uninjured arm around her shoulder and she shuddered. She must be freezing and his vampiric body could offer her no warmth. 'My god, you're freezing,' she gasped.

He grimaced. 'Yes. Did you think I'd be warmer after trapsing around in the snow searching for you?'

She remained silent but there was a scowl on her face that he found quietly adorable. He had enough sense not to say those words out loud.

Under his direction, she helped him to the castle. He led her to a sitting room with a large fireplace. 'I need a fire, and water and a cloth,' he told the castle. The fire burst to life and a bowl of warm water and a cloth appeared on the table. Alaric dropped into a big armchair, perspiration on his forehead. He needed blood. From the source would heal him faster but the blood the castle could provide would suffice. He didn't want to drink in front of her, he'd scared her enough for one night.

'You must have lost a lot of blood,' Belle said, and she knelt beside him to rip his sleeve. The wound was not bleeding anymore, but it was inflamed and oozing still. It pulsed with a heat that was unnatural for his cold body.

'We have to get you warm,' she muttered, casting around for something she could wrap him in.

He placed a hand on her shoulder, stilling her. 'You can't,' he said ruefully.

She studied his pale face, that same searching expression, the slight tilt of her head. 'Why?' she asked slowly.

He sighed. He couldn't keep it from her any longer.

'You must have noticed there was something a little different about those wolves in the forest.'

Belle nodded slowly, letting out a long breath as if she'd been trying to not to think about it. 'Yes. They were werewolves, weren't they?'

'You know of them?' he asked, surprised.

'I've read about them in stories. They weren't supposed to be real.'

'You're taking it better than I expected.'

'I saw that man transform. How am I supposed to deny his existence when I saw it with my own eyes?' she asked dubiously.

'True enough.'

'And you? What are you?' she asked, her eyes trained on him as she waited eagerly for his answer. She was holding her breath. Was she afraid to know what he was? He had been afraid to tell her all this time. What would she think when he told her?

'I think you already know,' he said and he braced himself for her fear, for the look in her eye that screamed monster.

There was no turning back now. He would have to tell her everything and if she rejected him now, there was no hope for him.

CHAPTER 9

Belle

In truth, she had already guessed what he was, though she had tried to deny it. There were too many signs for it to be merely coincidence; his pale skin, the coldness of his touch, the fangs, and his disappearing act when she pricked her finger. It explained his strength and speed and that portrait in the west wing. It explained why she only ever saw him at night. The more she thought about it, the more evidence there was to support her theory.

'You're a vampire,' she breathed.

He nodded sadly. 'And werewolf claws are not easy on a vampire. If I had been bitten, we wouldn't even be having this conversation. I suppose it makes sense that it would take a monster to kill a monster.'

Maybe he was a vampire, a monster, but he had also shown her kindness, and technically he did save her life. Although he was also the reason her life was in danger in the first place. But perhaps being a vampire and being a monster were not one and the same. She knew plenty of people who could pass as monsters better than Alaric.

She tilted her head as she looked up at him, as if trying to find the answers in his face. Try as she might, she couldn't see a monster there. He had scared her before, but if he hadn't lost his temper…

'How do you heal a wound like this?' she asked, doubting the water and wash cloth that had been laid out would be sufficient.

'I need to feed,' he said, refusing to look at her.

She felt only sympathy as she looked at Alaric now. He was clearly ashamed of what he was. It must have been so hard for him, trapped in this place, despising what he was. She was sure in that moment, he was not a monster.

But he needed to heal and to do that he needed blood.

Making up her mind, Belle squared her shoulders then held her wrist out to him. 'Then, you should feed,' she said, with all the bravery she could muster.

His head turned to her then, his eyes searching hers. He was much paler than usual, weak from the wound, and still he hesitated. 'Why?'

'You saved my life, and now I will return the favour,' she said and pushed her wrist at him again.

'This never would have happened if you hadn't run

away,' he said sullenly.

Belle quirked an eyebrow at him. 'Don't pretend that you didn't play a part in this. Now, hurry up, my arm is getting tired,' she said stubbornly, pushing her wrist towards him.

A small smile brushed Alaric's lips for a moment before he wrapped his cold fingers around her wrist and brought it to his lips. There was a sharp pain as his teeth sank into her flesh which was quickly replaced with a feeling of pleasure like she had never experienced before. It raced through her veins, speeding her heartbeat, and sparking a heat deep in her core. Before she could stop it, a moan escaped her lips.

Alaric pulled away in shock, letting her arm fall from his grasp. 'You – '

Her chest heaved with shallow breaths and she felt a deep disappointment that Alaric had stopped. His wound had healed completely, but now he was looking at her in shock. Did he not feel anything at all while he was feeding from her? Did all the people he fed from feel that same pleasure? Jealousy began to cloud her heart. She didn't want anyone else to know that feeling, she wanted him all to herself.

Alaric passed her the cloth, careful not to touch her, then put some distance between them, standing in front of the fireplace, resting one hand on the mantle, staring into the flames, preoccupied with thoughts Belle could barely guess at.

But she wasn't ready to let things end where they

were. He had ignited a need in her core that demanded to be filled. She refused to let him push her away. She put the cloth aside and stood up. She would not be so easily ignored. She reached back and began unfastening her dress with deft fingers. The sound of rustling fabric caused Alaric to look at her again and she slowly slipped the sleeve off one shoulder, revealing her smooth, porcelain skin, aware that his eyes were following her every movement.

'What are you doing?' Alaric asked. There was no emotion in his voice but his eyes showed her all she needed to know and she slid the other sleeve off and let the dress fall to her feet.

Alaric's spine stiffened and his body stilled completely. His gaze was hard but there was a flicker of something else, something she could recognise anywhere: desire. 'Belle, don't,' he said, but there was no conviction in those words, as if he was saying what he felt he should, not what he wanted.

'Why?' she asked, feigning innocence as she looked up at him with hooded eyes. 'Am I not to your taste?' The corner of her lips curled up into a seductive smile.

His eyes raked over her body, drinking in every inch of exposed skin. She stepped over the fabric at her feet, her movements slow and deliberate. Alaric remained silent and still, but he couldn't pull his eyes away. She took another step forward, the firelight dancing across her ivory skin, illuminating her shape beneath her slip. She enjoyed the way his eyes lingered on her, the way he seemed unable to look away. She pushed the remaining fabric from her shoulders, letting it slide down her arms and onto the floor. Alaric's breath hitched in his throat, his Adam's apple bobbing as he swallowed hard, his eyes drawn to her plump breasts. Her nipples hardened under his gaze and the muscles in her core clenched with need. She could feel herself growing wet for him and she ran her tongue over her bottom lip before biting down on it as the feeling intensified.

'Perhaps you prefer this?' she asked sensually and stepped towards him once again, closing the distance between them.

'You should stop,' Alaric said, his voice rough.

Belle placed a hand on his chest. 'You know,' she said, flicking her eyes up to meet his as she slowly slid her hand down his torso, coming to stop on his stiff erection. 'Your body is much more honest than your words, my lord.'

'Most girls would blush at the thought of doing what you are now,' Alaric said, gliding the back of his fingers along her jawline.

'I'm not most girls,' she said and a wicked smile crossed her lips. 'Shall I show you what girls like me do?' she asked, though she didn't care to hear his answer. Before he could say a word, she undid his pants, sliding them down his legs as she dropped to her knees before him. She took him in her mouth, slowly sliding her lips further down his shaft and he hissed out a breath in surprise. He entwined his fingers in her hair and Belle felt satisfaction welling up inside her as she continued to pleasure him, knowing by the way he was breathing that she had him right where she wanted him.

Suddenly, he forced her to stop, pulling her to her feet. A twinge of disappointment lasted only a second before he crushed his lips to hers, his kiss hungry and all consuming. She wrapped her arms around his neck and he deepened the kiss, caressing her tongue with his own. Each moan that escaped from her only seemed to stoke his hunger and she could feel him losing control, giving into his desire.

Belle's hand moved deftly to unbuttoning his shirt and Alaric quickly rid himself of his clothing. He lifted her into his arms and she wrapped her legs around him, eager to feel him against her centre. He pressed her back firmly against the wall and moved his lips to her jaw and down her neck and she moaned loudly as her body filled with a longing that could not be ignored. She could feel the slick head of his cock against her entrance and as the seconds ticked by, her longing turned into a need that she was desperate to sate, her muscles clenching in anticipation.

'Alaric, please,' she whimpered, her breathing ragged. She needed him inside her, it was all she could think about.

Instead of giving her what she wanted, he carried her to the rug in front of the fire. Her frustration and need tangled together and she wondered if he was taunting her on purpose. He laid her on the floor, hovering over her, his cock brushing teasingly against her clitoris.

'You are a monster,' she accused breathily.

A devilish smile touched his lips before he finally gave in, pushing into her gently, as if he was afraid to break her.

'More,' she begged, voice dripping in want. But Alaric continued to take his time, his lips grazing her breast, sucking at her taut nipple until she cried out and her muscles clenched around him. Finally, when she felt she couldn't bear it any longer, he relented, gripping her hips and pulling her hard against him. He thrust into her faster, harder, as her nails dug into his back and her voice filled the room.

Her muscles began to tighten around him as the pressure built unbearably within her. He sank his fangs into the nape of her neck, hot blood mingling with the sensation of his hot mouth clamped around her throat and that pleasure began coursing through her veins again like liquid fire, causing her whole body to tremble beneath him, pushing her over the edge. Alaric thrust into her a final time, deeper than ever before and he let out a guttural growl as he came with her.

They stayed that way, entangled by the fireplace until their breathing became less ragged. Alaric ran his fingers over the bite on her neck, and she saw the guilt forming in his eyes.

'Don't,' she said and Alaric looked at her quizzically. 'Don't you dare apologise.' She wasn't going to let him ruin this moment with a guilt he had no reason to feel. She had never felt so entirely satisfied in all her life, never felt so connected with another living soul as she did now with Alaric.

A soft smile touched his lips. He laid on his back, looking up at the ceiling. 'You are definitely not like most girls,' he said, a warm affection in his voice that Belle had never heard before.

She wanted to hear it again.

She wrapped her arm around him and placed her head on his chest. Feeling a subtle and contented happiness she had not felt in a very long time, she drifted into unconsciousness.

CHAPTER 10

Alaric

Alaric listened to the sound of Belle's breathing as she slept on him by the fire. He couldn't remember a time he'd ever felt this way about anyone. How easily she'd managed to find her way into his heart. She mumbled something unintelligible in her sleep and he smiled to himself. He should put her to bed but he wasn't ready to say goodbye to her yet.

He lifted her into his arms, careful not to wake her, but this time he took her to his bed in the west wing, to the bed he hadn't slept in for a hundred years. He'd tried so hard to keep her out, to keep her from seeing what he truly was. He knew he couldn't keep it from her forever but he'd hoped he could ease her into it. But that hadn't exactly gone to plan. Even so, she had accepted him anyway.

He tucked her into his bed and looked down at her for a moment, his heart warming at the sight. This is where she belongs, the thought came unbidden to his mind but it felt right. He climbed under the covers with her and she snuggled into him, despite the coldness of his skin.

'I'm afraid that if I fall asleep you will disappear like a dream when I wake,' he whispered softly as he stroked her hair.

As if she could hear him beneath the fog of sleep, she gripped him a little tighter. He had never been in love before but he was sure that this was it. Suddenly the hundred years he'd waited for her felt like a trifle. Belle was worth the wait.

The predawn light began to brighten the sky and with a heavy sigh, Alaric pulled away from her, despite the aching loneliness that sprung up in her absence. This was how it had to be for now. He opened his secret room and took one final look at her sleeping face before shutting himself away for the day.

He knew that one day soon he would never have to leave her side again.

CHAPTER 11

Belle

When Belle woke, she found herself in a big bed, but it wasn't her bed. It was the bed in the west wing, the place Alaric had forbidden her to go. A smile touched her lips at the thought of being granted access to a place he kept so private. But the smile faded when she realised that she was there alone.

As she mulled over the meaning of Alaric's absence, she noticed the sun was high in the sky and she realised it was already noon. If he was a vampire, did that mean he couldn't be in the sunlight? There were so many questions she should have asked him last night. Like why his bite had elicited such a pleasurable reaction, she hadn't expected that.

She spotted some clothing on a chair in the room. It had been placed there neatly and a smile came to

Belle's lips. It didn't feel like he'd abandoned her. After dressing, she found her way to the dining room again, and once again the table had been set with food for one. With a sigh, she sat and sullenly ate the offering of pancakes and bacon. Was she really going to have to wait the whole day before she could see him? She had so many questions burning in her mind.

Patience wasn't exactly one of her virtues.

The hours ticked slowly by and Belle found herself watching the sunset on the balcony of the west wing. Staring into the distance, she tried to put her thoughts in order. It wasn't like her to pine after a man. Maybe the loneliness of isolation was affecting her more than she'd realised. But then, she'd never met a man like Alaric before. Her fingers absently brushed the bite mark on her neck. Perhaps she should have been afraid of him but she couldn't imagine him ever hurting her. It didn't seem to be in his nature.

'Does it hurt?' Alaric's voice suddenly broke through her thoughts.

Belle spun around, her heart racing at the sound of his voice. 'Where have you been all day?' she asked, trying to feign innocence but the twitch at the corner of Alaric's lips told her that she'd failed.

'Did you miss me?' he asked.

Belle scowled at him. 'Why would I miss you?' she asked and turned her attention to the now velvet-black sky. She had missed him, which was entirely ridiculous. She'd only been without him half a day. This man was doing things to her that no other man had ever been able to.

Alaric wrapped his arms around her, pulling her close to him, and rested his chin on her shoulder. 'I know you missed me,' he said, his voice a low rumble that sent a pleasurable shiver through her body. Knowing full well that she was pouting, she said nothing because he was right.

'I was…asleep,' he said hesitantly. 'I've been told that when I sleep, I appear as a corpse. I didn't want to frighten you.'

A sense of guilt nestled painfully in her chest. There was so much about him that she didn't yet understand. 'I did miss you,' she said, relenting. She was rewarded with a tender kiss on her cheek that brought a smile to her lips. 'How did you become a vampire?' she asked.

Alaric let out a sigh and his arms tightened around her waist. 'It was a hundred years ago.'

'A hundred years? You've been here alone that long?' she asked, surprise clear in her voice. She couldn't imagine being trapped and alone for that long. How had he not gone mad?

Alaric nodded. 'A woman came to the castle, she was beautiful but there was something about her that I didn't trust. She hoped to marry me, but I turned her down. When she realised that she wasn't going to get what she wanted, she cursed me to an eternity as a monster, only living in the dark of night and she trapped me in this castle.

'My mother called for a witch, Delphine, who she thought could help me. Delphine said it was impossible to break the curse of another witch, but she could alter it. She gave me a dead rosebush and told me that the woman who made it bloom would be able to lift the curse, if she could love me despite my monstrous form.'

Belle turned her head to look back at him, eyes wide as realisation hit. The night she had gone to the west wing, she'd seen a rose bloom on the dead rosebush. Did that mean she was supposed to break his curse? How could she tell him that she didn't know how to do that?

Alaric smiled softly at her and his eyes filled with more warmth than she had ever experienced before. 'I had given up hope that you would find me,' he said.

A blush rose to Belle's cheeks and she dropped her gaze. Her heart raced even as she wondered how he could say such a thing with a straight face. She heard him chuckle and she pouted.

Suddenly, Alaric's head snapped up, his body becoming still as stone.

'What is it?' she asked, looking at him with concern.

'Someone is here.'

She looked in the direction that had drawn Alaric's attention, but she couldn't see or hear anything. 'Are you sure? I thought no one knew about this place?'

'They shouldn't,' he said, his brow furrowing.

An angry voice echoed through the cold night air,

followed by a loud, relentless banging. 'Open this door, monster!' a man yelled.

Belle stiffened. She knew that voice, but how the hell had he found his way to the castle. How had he even known? God, her father must have said something to the idiot. She thought she'd dealt with that problem with her very public rejection.

'You know who that is?' Alaric asked, his voice dark.

Belle sighed. She wanted the ground to open up and swallow her. It was certainly not a conversation she'd intended to have with Alaric. 'Unfortunately. His name is Gaston and he kind of…proposed to me.'

'Oh? And what answer did you give him?' There was a warning in his voice that ought to frighten her, since he was a vampire, but she found his jealousy thrilling. Not that she could act on it with Gaston banging down the door.

'Does he seem like the kind of man who would listen to a thing I say? I told him no and here he is, no doubt thinking that if he rescues me I won't be able to turn him down again,' she said, screwing her nose up in disgust.

'You're mine now, he cannot have you,' Alaric said, his arms tightening around her possessively.

She turned around in his arms and looked up at him. 'I don't want him to have me,' she said.

Alaric placed his finger under her chin. 'Good,' he said before claiming her lips passionately, as if he were claiming her.

The yelling continued, ruining their perfect moment, and Alaric finally released her with a frustrated sigh. 'I will get rid of him. Wait here.'

As he stepped away, Belle grabbed his wrist to stop him. 'Be careful.'

He quirked an eyebrow, a confident smirk tugging at his lips. 'I'm a vampire remember?' Before she could protest, Alaric had disappeared with inhuman speed.

'Shit,' she muttered, and she headed for the castle entrance as fast as humanly possible.

CHAPTER 12

Alaric

It was sweet of Belle to worry about him, but unnecessary. He hadn't dealt with human intruders very often, though he had dealt with the werewolves on the boarder, and they were far more challenging.

But this would be much more satisfying.

The man who had come to ruin his perfect evening with Belle, Gaston, she called him, was a big, burly-looking man. He wore expensive clothing and his hair was styled without a single strand out of place. He had a square jaw and was a few good inches taller than Alaric himself. But he had faced worse. This pretty boy was all show, he was sure of that.

'Come out and face me, monster!' Gaston, shouted, a vein bulging in his neck as his temper raged. To think such a loud, obnoxious creature thought to be worthy of his Belle.

'There's no need to shout, human,' Alaric said darkly, enjoying playing the part of the monster for the first time in a very long time.

'I know you have Belle,' Gaston snarled. 'Release her or I'll run you through.' He brandished a sword at Alaric, the blade glinting menacingly in the moonlight.

Alaric smirked and titled his head. 'Will you now? Tell me, why should I release her to you?'

'She is my fiancé,' Gaston spat with all the confidence of a man telling the truth, and yet Alaric knew that he was not.

'Funny, she told me that she rejected you,' Alaric said slowly. He was provoking the man, yes, but he had it coming. How dare this fool try to lay claim to what was his. A lesson would need to be taught if he would not back down, and oh how Alaric hoped he would not back down.

Gaston's face twisted with rage and he lunged for Alaric, who dodged the attack easily and thrust his fist into the man's face. With a satisfying crunch, Gaston's nose broke and blood poured from it as he howled in pain.

'Come now, human, I thought you were going to run me through,' Alaric said, a triumphant smile on his face.

Belle chose that moment to run outside.

Alaric clicked his tongue in irritation. Why couldn't she just stay put? He would handle the moron and she would be safe. Now he would need to ensure her safety as he fought her would-be lover. Not that it would make this much harder but he wasn't keen for her to see him behaving as the monster she claimed he wasn't.

He hoped she would understand if it meant she didn't have to go back with that brute.

'Belle!' Gaston shouted desperately when he saw her. 'Quickly, get away from here.'

Alaric snarled and pushed Belle behind him protectively. But she merely placed her hand on his arm and he knew that he had to let her do what she would or she would resent him for it. He wasn't keen on either option but he relented and let her stand beside him.

'I'm not leaving, Gaston,' she said firmly.

'What?' Gaston blinked in surprise and a silence hung in the air. Blood dripped down his face but he seemed to have forgotten it as he stared dumbfounded at Belle. 'You'd rather stay with a monster than marry me?'

'Any day of the week,' she said, her nose turning up in disgust.

'Why?' Gaston asked as if she were crazy, as if he could not conceive of a possible reason why she would choose anyone over him.

Belle's eyes shifted to Alaric, who was just as interested in her answer as Gaston. He'd tried not to push her but now that the question had been asked, he would not prevent her from answering. He needed to know.

'Because I love him,' she said, her voice soft and full of emotion.

Gaston's face twisted with rage and he ran towards Belle with a savage growl, a knife gripped tightly in his hand. Belle's eyes went wide but before she could react, Alaric was in front of her. The knife sliced through his arm and Alaric smiled a terrifying grin. He pulled the knife from his flesh and dropped it to the ground.

'That was a mistake,' he said, his voice dark and menacing. He picked Gaston up by the scruff and hurled him through the air. His body landed with a bone crunching crack on the stone path. He might live, if he was lucky, but Alaric would certainly do nothing to help that outcome.

'Alaric, are you alright?' Belle asked, voice thick with worry as she examined the wound. Though his shirt was soaked with blood, the wound itself had already healed.

'I'm fine,' he said dismissively. It wasn't him that he was worried about. He pulled her into his arms and held her tightly.

'You're the one who got hurt, not me,' Belle protested, and chuckled under her breath.

'Did you forget that I'm immortal?' Alaric asked, stroking her hair. She looked up at him with a frown, that beautiful little pout that appeared when he teased her. He was in real trouble. He was going to illicit that reaction whenever he could.

He picked her up, catching her off guard as he smiled wickedly down at her. 'What's that look?' she asked.

'I intend to pick up where we left off,' he said, capturing her lips once more before taking her back into the safety of the castle.

Once inside, he could hear the crackle of a fire and he stiffened, listening intently but all he could hear was that fire. And a heartbeat, slow, steady and confident. He knew exactly who that was.

Belladonna.

She was early, six months early. That meant she knew about Belle. What would she do to her? If after a hundred years she was still intent on marrying him, she would not take kindly to a woman coming in to take her place.

'Alaric? What's the matter?' Belle asked, looking up at him with concern.

He placed her on the ground and kissed her forehead tenderly, achingly. He couldn't lose her now. He wouldn't. 'I need you to go to my room. In the bookcase, pull the yellow book and go inside the secret room.'

'You have a secret room?'

He clicked his tongue in frustration. 'Belle, I need you to do this. Promise me you will wait there until I come to get you.'

'Why? Who's here?'

'Someone very dangerous who I do not want you to meet. Please, just do as I say,' Alaric pleaded.

She contemplated for a moment before nodding once. She placed her hand on his cheek. 'Be careful.'

He nodded, kissed her head once more and watched as she walked towards the west wing. When she had disappeared from sight, he eyed the sitting room where Belladonna was waiting for him. He took a deep breath and headed inside.

'Belladonna, to what do I owe this unpleasant surprise?' he asked, his tone flat. He didn't like to provoke her but he had to act as if nothing had changed, and if nothing had changed, then he would still think that she had done the worst thing imaginable to him.

She glared at him from her place in front of the fire, her eyes dark and terrifying like a raging storm. 'Alaric, to think you would still be so rude to be when you are hiding such a precious prize,' she said, her voice like venom.

'What prize is that?'

She chuckled darkly. 'Don't play coy with me, little prince. Bring her to me and I will spare your life.'

'I won't.'

'Oh, you won't. Well, I don't need you to play nice. I will simply trap you here in this room and go and kill her anyway.'

'I won't let you touch her,' Alaric snarled.

'So, the little prince thinks he's in love, does he?' Belladonna cooed as she tapped her nails on the mantle, the firelight dancing on her skin, giving her a menacing appearance that chilled his soul. 'And yet, here you stand, still the monster I cursed you to be.'

'What do you want, Belladonna?'

'The same thing I have always wanted, my love,' she said softly, moving towards him. She placed her hand on his cheek, exactly where Belle had placed hers only moments ago. Where Belle's touch had felt warm and soothing, Belladonna's felt cold and terrifying. 'Come back to me,' she whispered.

Alaric pulled away from her. 'I was never yours and I never will be.'

Her face twisted into an ugly snarl and she swiped her claws at him, gauging his face. The wound bled for a few moments before healing and Alaric made sure to stay perfectly still, as if he were dealing with a feral tiger and not a woman capable of conscious thought.

'Then you have made your choice, and you will regret it,' she hissed.

'Stop!' Belle suddenly shouted, placing herself between Alaric and the witch. It was as if time had stopped. A wicked grin pulled at Belladonna's lips as she locked onto Belle with a predatory glare.

Why couldn't she just do as he asked? The precarious situation had just exploded in his face ad he didn't know how he was supposed to protect her now.

CHAPTER 13

Belle

The idea of running away and hiding while Alaric faced the danger alone left a bad taste in Belle's mouth. But he was stubborn and a lot stronger than she was, so she had agreed to his request, knowing full well that she was going to disobey him. He would learn soon enough that she was not the type of woman to simply obey.

Once she was sure he wasn't watching her anymore, she headed back the way she came, to the sitting room she heard voices coming from. She pressed herself against the wall, standing as still as she was able, straining her ears to listen to their conversation through the doorway.

'What do you want, Belladonna?'

So this was Belladonna, this was the witch who had cursed him. Even after a hundred years she wouldn't let him go. She felt an anger towards the woman like she had never felt before, and yet without her she never would have met Alaric.

She peered through the doorway, trying to stay hidden. Belladonna was beautiful, with a youthful complexion and silvery hair. She looked up at Alaric with lustful eyes and touched a hand to his cheek. 'Come back to me,' she said, her voice sultry.

A possessiveness took hold of Belle's heart, filling her with such a hatred. How dare she touch Alaric after what she had done to him. How dare she touch what did not belong to her.

'I was never yours and I never will be,' Alaric said, moving away from her.

That's right. Keep your hands off him, Belle thought viciously. She could take no more of this. She threw herself between Alaric and the witch who had cursed him. 'Stop!' she shouted, glaring at the woman who was looking more unhinged by the second. Her nails dripped with Alaric's blood, her hair was slipping from its tie and her eyes were wild.

'Belle! I told you to hide, you shouldn't be here,' Alaric said, panic in his voice.

'She wanted me, here I am,' Belle said, staring the woman down. She didn't care who this woman was or how powerful, Belle had never run from a fight in her life and she was not going to start now, not when something so important was at stake.

'She's brave,' Belladonna sneered, 'but stupid. You

can't challenge me, little girl, I have lived longer than you could imagine.'

'Maybe, but I'm not the one chasing a man who hasn't wanted me for a hundred years,' Belle countered. 'How sad for you.'

Was it smart to provoke an ancient, clearly crazy witch? Probably not. But angry people make mistakes, it was something she'd learnt very early in her life, thanks to her father's teachings.

Belladonna hissed and lunged for Belle, her claws ready to strike. Alaric pushed Belle aside and she hit the ground hard enough to knock the wind out of her. She forced herself to her feet as the two struggled violently. Belladonna's claws sunk into Alaric's flesh again but he couldn't seem to land a blow on her at all.

Belladonna threw Alaric across the room and lunged at Belle again. Belle cast around for a weapon, anything she could use, but Belladonna was on her, knocking her to the ground once more, straddling her so she couldn't move.

'I won't let you have him,' Belladonna shrieked and struck a blow to her rival's face.

The taste of blood filled Belle's mouth but she smiled up at Belladonna anyway. 'I already have,' she said triumphantly and she chuckled despite the situation.

Belladonna howled with rage and pulled her arm back to strike again when she was ripped from Belle. Alaric snarled viciously and Belladonna howled in frustration, it was like watching two wild animals fighting and a shiver of fear ran down Belle's spine. But she couldn't get distracted, she couldn't let this witch win. Not again. The flames in the fireplace danced merrily despite the tension in the room and as she stared into them, an idea came to her mind.

Belladonna lunged at Alaric and he braced for the attack. Belle crept around them, hoping not to draw attention to herself as she got into position. Alaric had blood dripping from his wounds and Belladonna seemed unscathed though she was breathing hard.

'Why can't you just let this go?' he asked.

'Never,' she sneered.

'Give it up, witch. You've lost,' Belle said. They both looked at her as if they'd forgotten she was there and Belle seized the opportunity. She shoved Belladonna with all her strength right into the fireplace. She pulled the fireguard across it, holding it shut as the flames consumed Belladonna's body greedily, licking and flicking at her skin as it sizzled on her bones. Her screams filled the room and the stench of burning flesh.

Alaric put his hand on hers, gently prying her fingers from the guard as she stared into the flames. A little part of her felt sick at what she had just done but a bigger part of her felt only relief.

Alaric pulled Belle into his arms, shielding her from the grizzly sight. He lifted her up into his arms and whisked her away at vampire speed, the air whipped around her as her stomach roiled in protest. When he put her down, they were in the west wing again, in his room. He looked into her face, concern etched in his own as he examined her injuries.

With the loss of adrenaline, Belle's cheek throbbed angrily and she was acutely aware of the blood that must be coating her teeth, making her look frightful.

'Why didn't you stay hidden?' he asked, gently bringing his fingers to her cheek. His icy touch was soothing against the swelling and she closed her eyes, leaning into it.

'I couldn't leave you to face her alone,' Belle said.

'She could have killed you.'

Oh, she definitely could have done that, and for a moment, Belle thought she really might. But she also knew that she couldn't leave Alaric's side at such a crucial moment, she would never leave him to fight his battles alone, no matter how bad the odds.

'But she didn't.'

Alaric pricked his finger on one fang, a tiny bead of blood pooled on his fingertip. He put it to her lips. 'This will heal you,' he said.

Belle looked at the wound hesitantly. It was weird, incredibly weird, but she didn't want to hurt his feelings. She accepted his offer and licked the tiny bead off his finger. Instantly she began to feel the pain subside, the swelling in her cheek went down and she looked up at Alaric in surprise.

'Better?' he asked with a gentle smile.

She nodded and his smile turned sad. 'What is it?'

'No, it's nothing. I don't want you to worry about anything right now,' he said, stroking her hair gently.

'Tell me,' she insisted, her heart aching. He had spent so long on his own, so long carrying this burden alone.

'I just thought I would be human again,' he said with a small shrug.

Belle reached up, resting her hand against his cheek. 'Alaric, whether you are a human or a vampire, I love you.' She pressed her lips to his, trying to pour all of her feelings into that kiss. She expected to be met with his usual icy touch, but instead his lips were warm. She pulled back, startled.

'What is it?' Alaric asked confused.

She pressed her fingers to his cheek once more and blinked in surprise. 'You're warm,' she said. As she looked at him, colour began to seep into his skin, as if he were coming alive again.

Alaric touched his face, then his chest as if he was feeling his own heartbeat. He took a deep breath and a disbelieving smile tugged at his lips. His fingers ran along his teeth and finally he looked at Belle, his expression happier than she had ever seen it before.

He pulled her into his arms, lifting her from the ground and spinning her around in his joy. 'You did it!' he said and he captured her lips in a passionate kiss. 'You set me free. How could I ever repay you?'

'Well, I can think of a few things,' she said, smiling

down at him, tears pricking her eyes. She pressed her lips to his once more revelling in his happiness as if it was her own.

'I love you, Belle, more than you could ever know,' he said and something in his eyes had changed. They were filled with a burning desire that awakened something deep in her core.

Alaric sat on the edge of the bed and pulled her onto his lap and pressed his lips to hers gently at first but as his desire grew, his lips began to kiss her greedily. His hand found the ties of her dress and pulled them slowly open, revealing bear skin. He ran his fingers down her spine, letting her feel the warmth that now radiated from his skin.

Belle gasped at the sensation and goosebumps raced across each inch of skin that he exposed. She could feel him growing firm between her legs and desire began to burn in her core.

He cupped her face in his hands and slipped his tongue into her mouth. Belle's fingers deftly undid the buttons on his shirt. Her hands explored the firm muscles beneath the fabric, enjoying the warmth of his skin on hers and her longing built within her, growing steadily more unbearable.

Alaric kissed his way down her neck, nipping at her skin, and she moaned against him. He pulled the dress over her head, throwing it to the floor, exposing every inch of her. He took her tight nipple in his mouth, running his tongue along it. Belle's fingers tangled in his hair and she pulled him to her firmly, throwing her head back and allowing her voice to echo through the room.

He was so hard against her now, her body quivered with want, with anticipation. Unable to take it any longer, she reached between her legs, undoing his pants. She pulled him out, running her hand along the length of him.

'Impatient, are we?' he growled.

Belle ignored him. She pushed her underwear aside, then looked deep in his eyes as she pushed her hips down, sliding down his shaft. Her eyes fluttered shut as she moaned in pleasure, her body eagerly accepting all of him. She began moving her hips up and down as slow as she dared, intending to drive him as mad as he had threatened to drive her.

His fingers dug into her hips and he sighed in pleasure. She could tell what he wanted, but she refused to give in to him, refused to speed up the rhythm, enjoying every twitch of his body as his desire grew.

'You're abusing your power,' he said, voice rough. He stood up, lifting her with him, careful not to break their connection. He laid her on the bed, pinning her arms above her head with his large hand. 'My turn,' he growled. He thrust into her hard.

'Alaric, yes!' she cried out, her voice breaking the last of Alaric's resolve.

He crushed his lips to hers hungrily, his hips

rocking against her hard and fast. The pleasure built in her core with every thrust until finally the dam bust and waves of pleasure wracked her body, shuddering through her, pulsating around him. The sensation pushed him over the edge and he let out a guttural growl as he pushed himself deep inside her.

He laid down beside her and propped himself up on one arm. There was so much love in his eyes as he gazed down at her and she wondered for a moment if it was possible to die of happiness.

He wrapped his arm around her, pulling her close. She nestled into his embrace. 'What will you do now that you're human again?' she asked.

'I think I'll plant a garden full of roses, for my wife, the woman who saved me,' Alaric said with a wistful smile.

'You're wife?' Bell asked in surprise, her eyes flicking up to meet his.

'You don't think I'm letting you go now, do you?' he asked, a wicked smile pulling at his lips.

Belle smiled back at him and as he kissed her lovingly, she thought of the rose garden that he would plant for her and how those flowers would always remind her of this moment. She sighed contentedly as the firelight danced around them knowing that this was where she was meant to be.

EPILOGUE

Belle

Belle walked through the rose garden Alaric had planted for her, a soft smile on her lips. He had taken such pains to make sure it was perfect before revealing it to her. He had caught her many times trying to sneak in before it was finished and punished her in the most delicious ways.

She brushed the petals of one of the flowers, her ring sparkling in the early morning light. She was still getting used to it sitting on her finger. Marriage was something that she had thought of often enough, but she never really thought of it applying to her. She'd never really considered it for anyone other than Alaric.

The wedding itself had been small, Alaric didn't know many people and Belle didn't have many she wanted at the ceremony. It was intimate and perfect. But now they were to leave. She knew that Alaric was excited and she was, too, but she felt as if she would miss the castle. She knew they wouldn't be gone forever, but the castle had come alive when Alaric's curse had broken. Teams of staff now served, with the castle's enchantment gone, and it seemed to make Alaric happy to see it full of life again.

Delphine had altered the memories of the townsfolk and now all remembered their prince, only the royal family knew his true story and Belle was glad that his cousins had welcomed him with open arms while allowing him to live his life as he chose. She supposed that Alaric wanting nothing to do with the throne made the decision easy for them. He only wanted to be free.

And he had chosen to travel the world.

It was something she had never thought she would be able to do, as a woman, but with her husband she could go wherever she wanted. And while the idea excited her, she knew that she would look forward to coming home, to their home, and spending the rest of her life with the man she loved.

Strong arms wrapped around her. 'Are you ready to go, love?' Alaric asked and pressed a kiss to her cheek.

'Yes.'

He took her hand and led her to the carriage that awaited them. She knew this was a big moment for him. For the first time in a century, he was leaving the home that had become his prison. And when they returned, they would make it a home once more.

ABOUT THE AUTHOR

Lorelei Johnson is an Australian author who writes tantalising romances that will leave you wanting more.

While Lorelei typically writes paranormal romance, she will sometimes stray from that path to venture into the unexpected.

In her collection you'll find a variety of seductive romances featuring swoon-worthy men and feisty women. You're bound to find the HEA you're looking for.

Lorelei Johnson

BOOKS BY LORELEI JOHNSON

<u>Tantalising Tales Collection</u>

My Sweet Cinderella

Scarlett and the Wolf

Beauty and the Beast

The Touch of Snow

The Little Mermaid

Summoned by the Piper

<u>Loved by the Zodiac</u>

Loved by Aries

Embraced by Scorpio

Lorelei Johnson